This Little Tiger book belongs to:

_____

_____

_____

_____

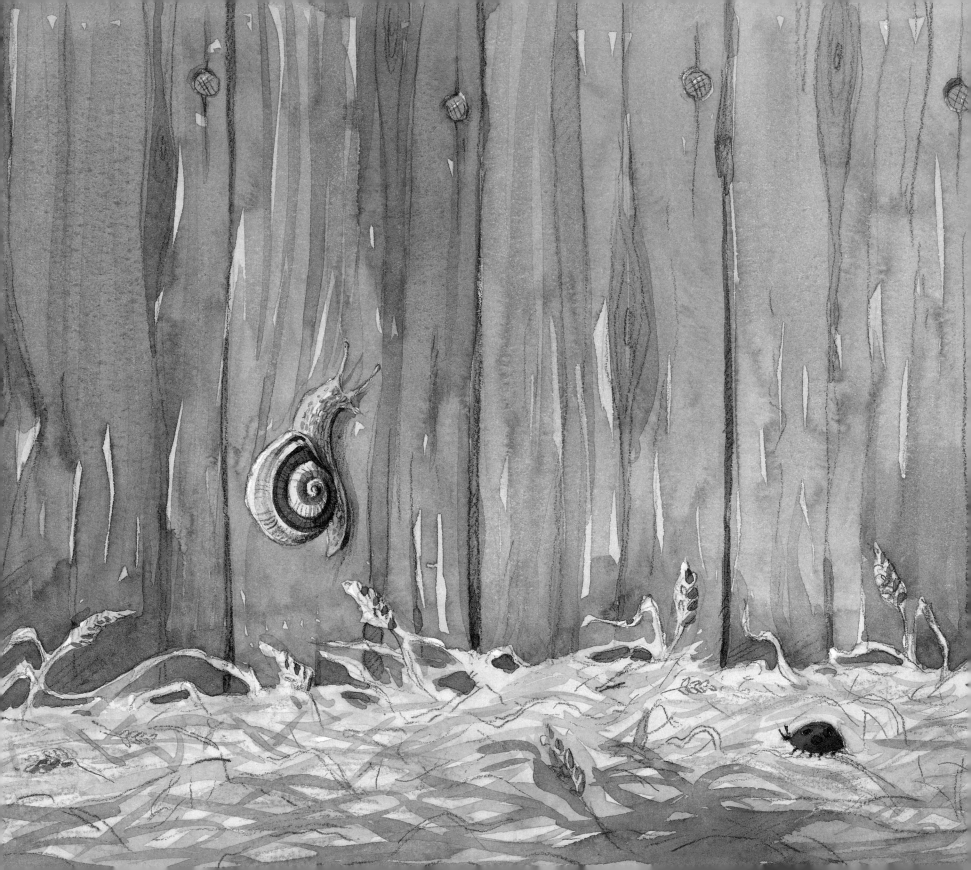

for Melanie,
with love
~SR

for Hannah,
with love
~SL

LITTLE TIGER PRESS
An imprint of Magi Publications
1 The Coda Centre, 189 Munster Road, London SW6 6AW
www.littletigerpress.com
First published in Great Britain 2004
This edition published 2005

Text copyright © Shen Roddie 2004
Illustrations copyright © Steve Lavis 2004
Shen Roddie and Steve Lavis have asserted their rights to be
identified as the author and illustrator of this work under
the Copyright, Designs and Patents Act, 1988

A CIP catalogue record for this book is available
from the British Library

ISBN 1 85430 965 X

Printed in China

2 4 6 8 10 9 7 5 3

You're Too Small!

Shen Roddie

illustrated by

Steve Lavis

LITTLE TIGER PRESS
London

Pip woke up all warm and tingly as a dot of sunshine touched his nose.

He peered out of the window. "Everyone's busy!" he piped. "I'll run down and help."

Pig was pushing a barrow
of marrows.

"I'll help you," said Pip.

"Better not," said Pig. "You're
too small. You'd get squashed."

Nearby, Goat was stacking hay.

"Can I help?" asked Pip.

"No thank you," said Goat.

"You're too small. You'd get lost."

Pip ran off and found Cow. He was painting a wall.

"I can help!" said Pip.
"I don't think so," said
Cow. "You're too small.
You'd never reach
the top."

"Well," thought Pip, "if I'm too small to help, I'll just have to go and play!"

He skipped off into the fields where he met Rabbit, flying a kite.

"Can I have a go?" asked Pip, watching the kite wiggling in the clouds.

"No!" said Rabbit. "You're too small. You'd get blown away!"

Pip looked at himself.
He looked at his big paws,
his round belly and his long tail.
  "I don't look small to me!" he
said. "I look just right! I'll ask
Goose. She won't think I'm
too small."

"Too small for what?" asked
Goose.
  "I don't know," said Pip. "But
maybe I'm the right size to sit
on your eggs. After all, you
don't look very big yourself!"

Goose took a deep breath.
Then she stood up . . . taller . . .
and taller . . .
 "Pip," she said, peering
down at him. "I would love
you to sit on my eggs but
you wouldn't cover them at
all. You are just too small!"

"Oh dear," said Pip. "I think I'll
go back to bed and start again
tomorrow. Perhaps I'll have
grown some more by then."

Pip walked slowly back to
the barn. But when he got
to the door . . .

. . . there was a big hubbub! All his friends were there, banging on the door. "Pig came to tell us dinner was ready and the door slammed behind him. We're all locked out!" cried Rabbit. "And we're starving!" said Goose.

"I can help," said Pip.

"What can you do?" said the animals. "You're too small!"

"I don't have to be big to help," said Pip. And he disappeared . . .

. . . through a crack in the wall.
"I only need to be small enough!"
he called from inside. He heard
a loud cheer from outside.
"Hurray for Pip! Hurray!
Hurray! Hurray!"
But since dinner was
all ready . . .

. . . Pip hopped on to the table.
"There's another thing I'm not
too small for . . ." he smiled, as
he helped himself to the biggest,
plumpest puffed-up pie!

Then he hopped off the table,
unlocked the door . . . and let
his hungry friends in.
"Thank you, Pip!" they shouted.
"You're just the right size."
Pip smiled a big puffed-up
pie smile. But all he said was . . .

"BURP!"

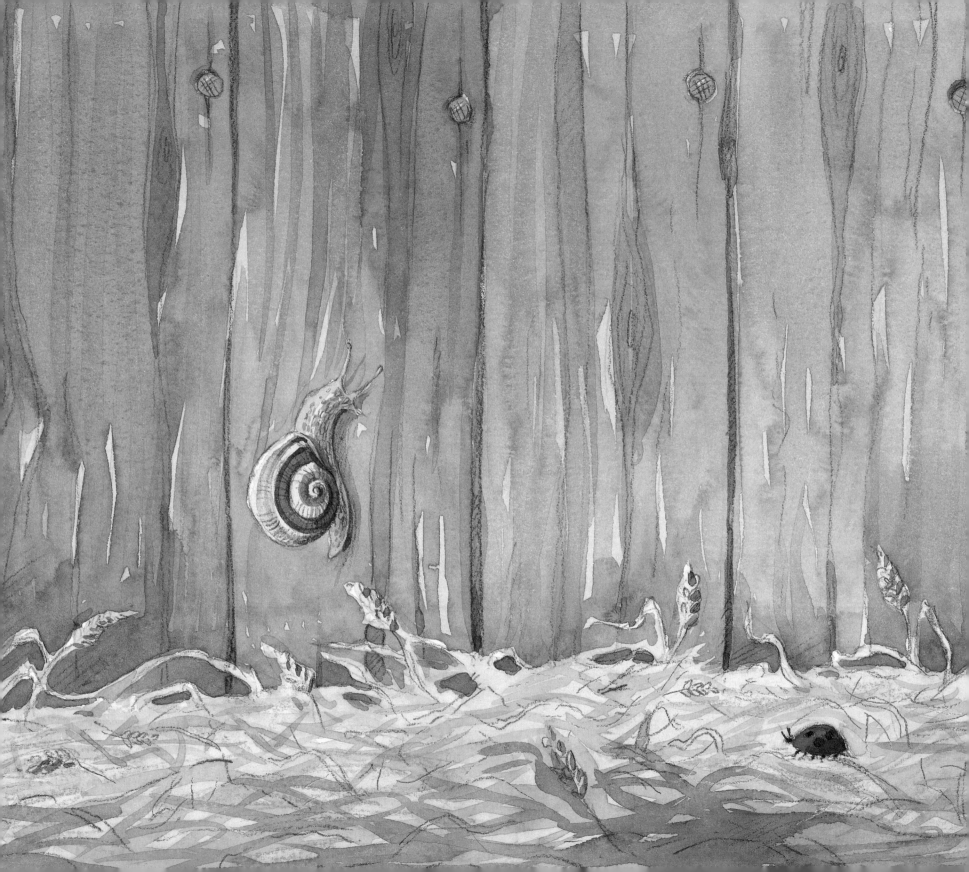

Fantastic reads from Little Tiger Press

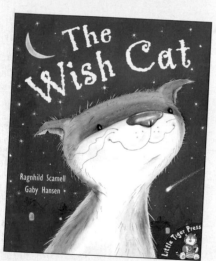

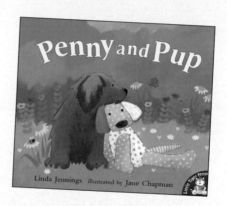

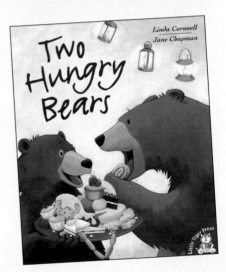

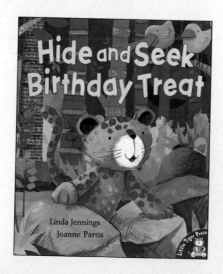

For information regarding any of the above titles
or for our catalogue, please contact us:
Little Tiger Press, 1 The Coda Centre,
189 Munster Road, London SW6 6AW, UK
Tel: +44 (0)20 7385 6333 Fax: +44 (0)20 7385 7333
E-mail: info@littletiger.co.uk
www.littletigerpress.com